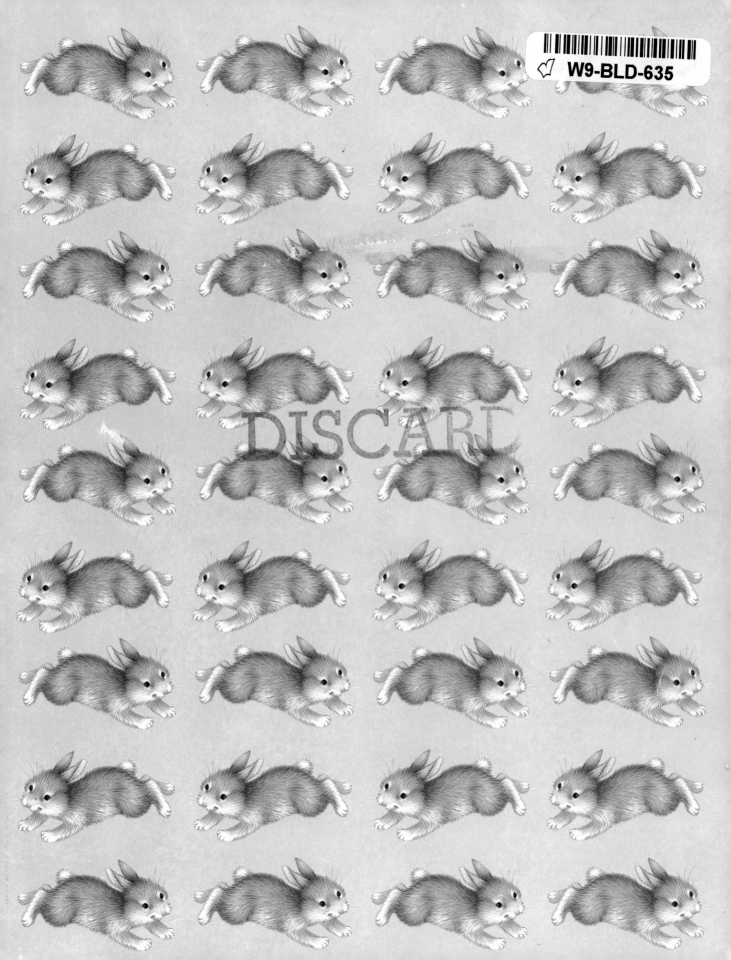

Margaret Wise Brown

BUNNY'S
NOISY BOOK

PICTURES BY Lisa McCue

HYPERION BOOKS FOR CHILDREN
NEW YORK

First Edition
1 3 5 7 9 10 8 6 4 2

Printed in Hong Kong by South China Printing Company, Ltd.

Library of Congress Cataloging-in-Publication Data
Brown, Margaret Wise, 1910−1952.
Bunny's noisy book/Margaret Wise Brown; illustrated by Lisa McCue.
p. cm.
Summary: A little bunny listens to noises all around him
and then makes some of his own.
ISBN 0-7868-0472-6 (alk. paper)—ISBN 0-7868-2428-X (lib. bdg.)
[1. Rabbits—Fiction. 2. Sound—Fiction.] I. McCue, Lisa, ill. II. Title.
PZ7.B8163Bu 2000
[E]—dc21   99-19024

For Kenny and Richard

Search every picture,
Search and you'll find,
I've hidden McCUE
thirteen times.
—L. M.

When he first woke up in the morning he didn't open his eyes. Why should he, that little bunny? He raised his ears without opening his eyes. He heard all the little quiet noises starting the morning around him.

First, what did he hear?

First, nothing.

Then there was sudden fluttering and chirping.

What was that?

Birds getting up out of their nests
and off the branches and beating their wings.
　　Far off—very far away—he heard a
Cock Cock Cock-a-doodle Doo!
　　What was that?

The little bunny opened his eyes, went up
the tunnel to his home, and out to see.

Sound came from the world above.
The little bunny heard a **bzzzzzzzz.**
What was that?

Yes. It was a bumblebee.

Two bumblebees.

Then the little bunny started on
a big green leaf and began to make a
little noise himself.

How was that?

Then he **stretched**.
And what kind of noise was that?

Then he **yawned**.

And what kind of noise was that?

Then he **scratched**.

And what kind of noise was that?

Then he **sneezed**.
And what kind of noise was that?

And then he went hop-hop over to a
big pink clover that was buzzing with bees.

All day long he ate
big pink clover.

At the end of the day, the sun went down.
But could the little bunny hear that? **No!**

But he could hear the little noises of the night
beginning around him.
The wind began to blow louder and stronger.

Branches snapped.

And then there was an old familiar **thump**
as his mother banged her heels on the ground.

That meant run for home.
The old red fox was taking a stroll.
Time for little bunnies to be safe
in their hole.

And he popped down the rabbit hole just as
the fox barked.

He wiggled his nose and sniffed the little
quick noise of a sniff.

How was that?

And he jumped into his little bed of leaves,
curled in a little fur ball, and tucked his paws
under him.

Then the little bunny sighed his little bunny sigh.

His ears fell down and he nodded over, sound asleep in his own warm hole in the big quiet night.